JESUS

TELL HIM WHAT YOU WANT

30 Days Inspiring devotional

Erica Moss

**Copyright © 2023 Erica Moss
All rights reserved.**

No part of this publication may be reproduced, distributed, or transmitted in any form or by any means, including photocopying, recording, or other electronic or mechanical methods, without the prior written permission of the publisher, except in the case of brief quotations embodied in critical reviews and certain other noncommercial uses permitted by copyright law. For permission requests, write to the publisher, addressed Attention: Permissions Coordinator, at the address below.
Cataloging-in-Publication date for this book is available from the Library of Congress.

Images used under license from Shutterstock.com and stock images.

Unless otherwise indicated, all Scripture quotations are taken from the Holy Bible, New International (NIV)® and King James (KJV) Versions®

ISBN: 978-1-961650-05-3 (Paperback)
ISBN: 978-1-961650-04-6 (eBook)
Printed in the United States of America.
Published in the United States by GeeMorgan Publishing LLC

First printing edition 2023.
All inquiries about this book can be sent to the author at
Ericamoss@geemorganpublishing.com or
hello@geemorganpublishing.com

For more information, or to book an event, visit the website:
www.geemorganpublishing.com
GeeMorgan Publishing LLC
19046 Bruce B Downs Blvd #1016,
Tampa, FL 33647
www.geemorganpublishing.com

TABLE OF CONTENTS

Opening Page 1

Dedication 2

Day 1 - Have A Little Faith 3

Day 2 – Strength 6

Day 3 - Living In Sin 9

Day 4 – Being Judgmental 12

Day 5 - Love 15

Day 6 – Help 18

Day 7 – Grateful 21

Day 8 – Boasting 24

Day 9 - Trust God's Time 27

Day 10 - Distress 30

Day 11 - Grace 33

Day 12 - Do Right By Others 36

Day 13 - Obedience 39

Day 14 - Blessed 42

Day 15 - Guidance 45

Day 16 – Wisdom 48

Day 17 - Put God First 51

Day 18 - A Relationship With The Lord 54

Day 19 - Pray 57

Day 20 - Signs From The Lord 60

Day 22 – Peace 66

Day 23 – Forgiveness 69

Day 24 - The Lord Is Everywhere 72

Day 25 - Distractions 75

Day 26 - Happiness 78

Day 27 - Heaven Is Real 81

Day 28 - Hell Is Real 84

Day 29 - Encouragement 87

Day 30 - Salvation 90

Commitment And Recommitment 93

Acknowledgments 94

OPENING PAGE

Trust in the Lord with all thine heart; and lean not unto thine own understanding. In all thy ways acknowledge Him, and He shall direct thy paths"

- Proverbs 3:5-6

DEDICATION

I dedicate this book to my mother, Betty Sue Johnson, her personality, wisdom, and strength, taught me to persevere through all life circumstances.

~ EM

DAY 1 - HAVE A LITTLE FAITH

"Now Faith is the substance of things hoped for, the evidence of things not seen"

- Hebrews 11:1

LIFE LESSON

In 2015, I made the decision to leave my job and move to Alaska to be with my husband. The uncertainty of when I would find employment again weighed heavily on my heart. In these moments of doubt, I turned to prayer, laying my concerns before the Lord. Miraculously, within three months of our arrival in Alaska, I was blessed with a position at The Alaska VA. This experience reminded me that even when we cannot discern God's plan, it is imperative to place our trust in Him. For He is always working behind the scenes in our favor.

PRAYER

Heavenly Father, I am profoundly grateful for both the blessings I see and those that are unseen. May my faith in You remain unshaken, trusting always in Your divine plan. **In Jesus' name, I pray, Amen.**

REFLECTION

As you meditate on today's scripture and lesson, what thoughts or feelings arise? How does this message resonate with your current life circumstances or past experiences? Take a moment to jot down your reflections below.

ACTION

Having reflected on today's message, what tangible steps can you take to apply this lesson in your daily life? Write down one or more actions you intend to take as a response.

_____

_____

_____

_____

_____

_____

_____

_____

_____

_____

_____

_____

_____

_____

_____

_____

DAY 2 – STRENGTH

"I can do all things through Christ which strengthens me."

- Philippians 4:13

LIFE LESSON

At the age of 55, my mother passed away due to Cirrhosis of the Liver. I was beside her, bearing witness to her final moments.

Rather than questioning the Lord Jesus in that heart-wrenching moment, I chose gratitude; I was thankful she was free from pain. Yet, as days turned into nights, the weight of her absence bore down on me. Recognizing the depth of my grief, I turned to prayer, seeking Jesus's comfort not just for me, but for my father and siblings as well. True to His promise, He bestowed upon us strength, healing, and grace.

PRAYER

Heavenly Father, thank You for your love and mercy and being my refuge during challenging periods in my life. Thank You for standing by my family and I, providing strength and solace. I will forever praise Your Holy name. **In Jesus' name, I pray, Amen.**

REFLECTION

As you meditate on today's scripture and lesson, what thoughts or feelings arise? How does this message resonate with your current life circumstances or past experiences? Take a moment to jot down your reflections below.

ACTION

Having reflected on today's message, what tangible steps can you take to apply this lesson in your daily life? Write down one or more actions you intend to take as a response.

DAY 3 - LIVING IN SIN

"For all have sinned, and come short of the glory of God."

- Romans 3:23

LIFE LESSON

As a result of man's fall from grace in the beginning, we all have been condemned to wear sins justifiable punishment. The world we live in holds many tangible whims and wants which we often chase after hoping to receive some genuine belonging in life. In my own personal experiences, I've found out they only lead to lustful desires and false fulfillments, casting sins ugly shadow. To truly live a life worthy of God's glory, we must shun our fleshly desires and turn to Jesus Christ, allowing Him to guide us on the path of righteousness and elevating our spiritual walk.

PRAYER

Heavenly Father, Almighty God, sustain me in moments of weakness and guide me towards Your eternal light. Forgive my sins, both those I recognize and those hidden from my sight. **In Jesus' name, I pray, Amen.**

REFLECTION

As you meditate on today's scripture and lesson, what thoughts or feelings arise? How does this message resonate with your current life circumstances or past experiences? Take a moment to jot down your reflections below.

_____

_____

_____

_____

_____

_____

_____

_____

_____

_____

_____

_____

_____

_____

_____

_____

_____

_____

ACTION

Having reflected on today's message, what tangible steps can you take to apply this lesson in your daily life? Write down one or more actions you intend to take as a response.

DAY 4 - BEING JUDGMENTAL

"Do not judge, or you too will be judged."

- Matthew 7:1

LIFE LESSON

It's a common pitfall: hastily forming opinions about others. Yet, none of us truly have the authority to judge. Only God, who sees the fullness of every heart and the features of every soul, holds that right. He sits high and looks low.

PRAYER

Heavenly Father, grant me the ability to see others with an open heart and not rely solely on my own perceptions. **In Jesus' Name, I pray, Amen.**

REFLECTION

As you meditate on today's scripture and lesson, what thoughts or feelings arise? How does this message resonate with your current life circumstances or past experiences? Take a moment to jot down your reflections below.

_____

_____

_____

_____

_____

_____

_____

_____

_____

_____

_____

_____

_____

_____

_____

_____

ACTION

Having reflected on today's message, what tangible steps can you take to apply this lesson in your daily life? Write down one or more actions you intend to take as a response.

_____

_____

_____

_____

_____

_____

_____

_____

_____

_____

_____

_____

_____

_____

_____

_____

DAY 5 - LOVE

"For God so loved the world, that He gave His only begotten Son, that whoever believes in Him should not perish, but have everlasting life."

- John 3:16

LIFE LESSON

When I look back over my life's journey, I am moved with tears when I realize the countless moments Jesus Christ has shown me unconditional love. Why? seems to be a reasonable question to bring clarity to living in this world pledged by sin. Haven't we all, at some point in our lives, just paused and marveled at the thought, "How have I made it thus far?" The answer is simple yet profound: it's God's unwavering love.

PRAYER

Heavenly Father, thank You for showing me Your constant, never changing love without bounds or conditions. Please continue to keep a shield of protection around me. **In Jesus' Name, I pray, Amen.**

REFLECTION

As you meditate on today's scripture and lesson, what thoughts or feelings arise? How does this message resonate with your current life circumstances or past experiences? Take a moment to jot down your reflections below.

_____

_____

_____

_____

_____

_____

_____

_____

_____

_____

_____

_____

_____

_____

_____

_____

_____

ACTION

Having reflected on today's message, what tangible steps can you take to apply this lesson in your daily life? Write down one or more actions you intend to take as a response.

_____

_____

_____

_____

_____

_____

_____

_____

_____

_____

_____

_____

_____

_____

_____

_____

DAY 6 – HELP

"I will lift up mine eyes unto the hills, from whence cometh my help. My help cometh from the Lord, which made heaven and earth."

- Psalms 121:1-2

LIFE LESSON

Every blessing, every achievement, and every possession we cherish is a testament to God's grace. We may labor diligently and strive for success, but it's essential to know that without the Lord's guidance and favor, the comforts, and accomplishments we enjoy would be beyond reach.

PRAYER

Heavenly Father, thank you for the bountiful blessings You've bestowed upon me, even when I don't deserve them. I take no honor unto myself giving you all the praise. **In Jesus' name, I pray, Amen**.

REFLECTION

As you meditate on today's scripture and lesson, what thoughts or feelings arise? How does this message resonate with your current life circumstances or past experiences? Take a moment to jot down your reflections below.

ACTION

Having reflected on today's message, what tangible steps can you take to apply this lesson in your daily life? Write down one or more actions you intend to take as a response.

DAY 7 – GRATEFUL

"Giving thanks always for all things unto God and the Father in the name of Our Lord Jesus Christ."

- Ephesians 5:20

LIFE LESSON

Gratitude should be our constant companion. At times we may take for granted the simple comfortabilities we have in life. While living in Alaska, I witnessed numerous homeless individuals braving the cold winters, searching for shelter, sustenance, and warmth. Observing their struggles deepened my appreciation for the blessings in my life.

PRAYER

Heavenly Father, I am extremely thankful for a roof over my head, clothes on my back, and food to eat. May Your blessings continue to cover those less fortunate than I. **In Jesus' name, I pray, Amen**.

REFLECTION

As you meditate on today's scripture and lesson, what thoughts or feelings arise? How does this message resonate with your current life circumstances or past experiences? Take a moment to jot down your reflections below.

_____
_____
_____
_____
_____
_____
_____
_____
_____
_____
_____
_____
_____
_____

ACTION

Having reflected on today's message, what tangible steps can you take to apply this lesson in your daily life? Write down one or more actions you intend to take as a response.

_____

_____

_____

_____

_____

_____

_____

_____

_____

_____

_____

_____

_____

_____

_____

_____

DAY 8 – BOASTING

"But, Let the one who boasts boast in the Lord. For it is not the one who commends himself who is approved, but the one whom the Lord commends."

- 2 Corinthians 10:17-18

LIFE LESSON

Ever come across the phrase, "sitting on a high horse"? When we elevate ourselves too much, the Lord Jesus reminds us of our true place. Whether we live in luxury, drive the latest car, or carry a prestigious title, we should never consider ourselves superior to others. It's vital to know whom we have obtained these comforts from.

PRAYER

Heavenly Father, may I always sing praises of You and never of my own accomplishments. **In Jesus' Name, I pray, Amen.**

REFLECTION

As you meditate on today's scripture and lesson, what thoughts or feelings arise? How does this message resonate with your current life circumstances or past experiences? Take a moment to jot down your reflections below.

_____

_____

_____

_____

_____

_____

_____

_____

_____

_____

_____

_____

_____

_____

_____

ACTION

Having reflected on today's message, what tangible steps can you take to apply this lesson in your daily life? Write down one or more actions you intend to take as a response.

DAY 9 - TRUST GOD'S TIME

"To everything there is a season, and a time for every purpose under heaven."

- Ecclesiastes 3:1

LIFE LESSON

God's timing often differs from our own. While we might yearn for something immediately, feeling it's our moment, the Lord Jesus knows when it's truly right for us. He may not respond according to our timeline, but He is always on time.

PRAYER

Heavenly Father, thank You for the moments You've taught me to wait and trust in Your perfect timing. I pray for continued patience as I place my trust in You. **In Jesus' Name, I pray, Amen.**

REFLECTION

As you meditate on today's scripture and lesson, what thoughts or feelings arise? How does this message resonate with your current life circumstances or past experiences? Take a moment to jot down your reflections below.

_____

_____

_____

_____

_____

_____

_____

_____

_____

_____

_____

_____

_____

_____

_____

_____

ACTION

Having reflected on today's message, what tangible steps can you take to apply this lesson in your daily life? Write down one or more actions you intend to take as a response.

_____

_____

_____

_____

_____

_____

_____

_____

_____

_____

_____

_____

_____

_____

_____

DAY 10 - DISTRESS

"Then Jesus said to his disciples, therefore, I tell you, do not worry about your life, what you will eat, or about your body, what you will wear."

- Luke 12:22

LIFE LESSON

Have you ever tossed and turned late in the midnight hours? The Lord Jesus encourages us to lay all our worries at His feet. He is acutely aware of our struggles, and His promise is clear: if He brings us to a situation, He will surely bring us through it.

PRAYER

Heavenly Father, Thank You for always being my provider, my lawyer when I feel judged, my healer in times of illness, a shelter in the times of a storm. **In Jesus' Name, I pray, Amen.**

REFLECTION

As you meditate on today's scripture and lesson, what thoughts or feelings arise? How does this message resonate with your current life circumstances or past experiences? Take a moment to jot down your reflections below.

_____

_____

_____

_____

_____

_____

_____

_____

_____

_____

_____

_____

_____

_____

_____

_____

ACTION

Having reflected on today's message, what tangible steps can you take to apply this lesson in your daily life? Write down one or more actions you intend to take as a response.

_____

_____

_____

_____

_____

_____

_____

_____

_____

_____

_____

_____

_____

_____

_____

_____

_____

DAY 11 - GRACE

"But in your great mercy, you did not put an end to them or abandon them, for you are a gracious and merciful God."

- Nehemiah 9:31

LIFE LESSON

At just 20 years old, I faced a life-altering diagnosis: a pulmonary embolism, a blood clot in my lungs. Spending several days in the hospital and undergoing six months of treatment made me grasp the gravity of my situation. But in my follow-up after those challenging months, the doctor revealed the clot had disappeared. It was a testament to the Lord Jesus' power as a healer, miracle worker, and a promise keeper.

PRAYER

Heavenly Father, I lift Your name on high because You are worthy to be praised. Thank You for the wonders You've done in my life and for the grace You shower upon me every day. **In Jesus' Name, I pray, Amen.**

REFLECTION

As you meditate on today's scripture and lesson, what thoughts or feelings arise? How does this message resonate with your current life circumstances or past experiences? Take a moment to jot down your reflections below.

ACTION

Having reflected on today's message, what tangible steps can you take to apply this lesson in your daily life? Write down one or more actions you intend to take as a response.

_____

_____

_____

_____

_____

_____

_____

_____

_____

_____

_____

_____

_____

_____

_____

DAY 12 - DO RIGHT BY OTHERS

"Bless those who curse you. Pray for those who mistreat you."

- *Luke 6:28*

LIFE LESSON

At the Alaska VA, I crossed paths daily with a colleague who often chose to ignore me. I chose to pray about the situation rather than hold a grudge. In an unexpected twist, a year later, as a supervisor, I found her name among applicants for a lead role in my department. Our past interactions came to mind, underscoring the importance of treating others with kindness and respect, no matter the circumstances.

PRAYER

Heavenly Father, thank You for instilling in me a heart of patience and love. Guide me to consistently treat others with kindness and fairness, as You would. **In Jesus' name, I pray, Amen.**

REFLECTION

As you meditate on today's scripture and lesson, what thoughts or feelings arise? How does this message resonate with your current life circumstances or past experiences? Take a moment to jot down your reflections below.

_____
_____
_____
_____
_____
_____
_____
_____
_____
_____
_____
_____
_____
_____
_____
_____

ACTION

Having reflected on today's message, what tangible steps can you take to apply this lesson in your daily life? Write down one or more actions you intend to take as a response.

DAY 13 - OBEDIENCE

"Children, obey your parents in everything, for this pleases the Lord."

- Colossians 3:20

LIFE LESSON

God cherishes obedience from His children. It doesn't matter if we're young or old, showing respect and honor to our parents is essential. Reflecting on my younger days, I regret the times I talked back to my mom, not fully grasping the weight of my actions. Now, with a deeper understanding of the Scriptures, I strive to live by its teachings and pass on these values to my own children.

PRAYER

Heavenly Father, thank You for granting me the wisdom to value obedience. May I always remain grounded in Your words passing them on to others. **In Jesus' Name, I pray, Amen.**

REFLECTION

As you meditate on today's scripture and lesson, what thoughts or feelings arise? How does this message resonate with your current life circumstances or past experiences? Take a moment to jot down your reflections below.

_____

_____

_____

_____

_____

_____

_____

_____

_____

_____

_____

_____

_____

_____

_____

_____

ACTION

Having reflected on today's message, what tangible steps can you take to apply this lesson in your daily life? Write down one or more actions you intend to take as a response.

_____

_____

_____

_____

_____

_____

_____

_____

_____

_____

_____

_____

_____

_____

_____

DAY 14 - BLESSED

"Every good and perfect gift is from above, coming down from the Father of the heavenly lights, who does not change like shifting shadows."

- James 1:17

LIFE LESSON

Today, if you opened your eyes and took a breath, know that it's a blessing from the Lord Jesus. It wasn't the alarm, the chime of a phone, or the call of the rooster. It was God's grace and love.

PRAYER

Heavenly Father, thank You for gifting me another day in Your grace. I pray for guidance to live each day in line with Your purpose. **In Jesus' Name, I pray, Amen.**

REFLECTION

As you meditate on today's scripture and lesson, what thoughts or feelings arise? How does this message resonate with your current life circumstances or past experiences? Take a moment to jot down your reflections below.

ACTION

Having reflected on today's message, what tangible steps can you take to apply this lesson in your daily life? Write down one or more actions you intend to take as a response.

DAY 15 - GUIDANCE

"I will instruct you and teach you in the way you should go. I will counsel you with my loving eye on you."

- Psalms 32:8

LIFE LESSON

Consider the path we tread. Without the wisdom and instruction of the Holy Bible, we are living by our own rules. The Bible isn't just a book; it's a compass, guiding us through life's journey.

PRAYER

Heavenly Father, thank You for going before me guiding my every step. May I always follow Your lead. **In Jesus' Name, I pray, Amen.**

REFLECTION

As you meditate on today's scripture and lesson, what thoughts or feelings arise? How does this message resonate with your current life circumstances or past experiences? Take a moment to jot down your reflections below.

_____
_____
_____
_____
_____
_____
_____
_____
_____
_____
_____
_____
_____
_____
_____
_____
_____
_____

ACTION

Having reflected on today's message, what tangible steps can you take to apply this lesson in your daily life? Write down one or more actions you intend to take as a response.

_____
_____
_____
_____
_____
_____
_____
_____
_____
_____
_____
_____
_____
_____
_____
_____

DAY 16 – WISDOM

"Ask and it will be given to you; seek and you will find, knock and the door will be opened to you."

- Matthew 7:7

LIFE LESSON

Initially, the words of the Bible felt elusive and hard to grasp for me. It felt like a puzzle with missing pieces. Yet, instead of being discouraged, I turned to prayer, seeking clarity, and understanding from the Lord. Over time, I began to immerse myself into the scriptures, picturing myself within its tales and lessons. Now, the Bible is my daily bread. When in doubt, turn to Him; He grants understanding and fills the gaps in our knowledge.

PRAYER

Heavenly Father, mold me to reflect Your wisdom. Gift me with understanding so I can share Your teachings with others. **In Jesus' Name, I pray, Amen.**

REFLECTION

As you meditate on today's scripture and lesson, what thoughts or feelings arise? How does this message resonate with your current life circumstances or past experiences? Take a moment to jot down your reflections below.

_____

_____

_____

_____

_____

_____

_____

_____

_____

_____

_____

_____

_____

_____

_____

ACTION

Having reflected on today's message, what tangible steps can you take to apply this lesson in your daily life? Write down one or more actions you intend to take as a response.

DAY 17 - PUT GOD FIRST

"But seek His wisdom and His righteousness, and all these things will be given to you as well."

- Matthew 6:33

LIFE LESSON

Our Creator asks for unwavering devotion, placing Him above all material and worldly desires. The allure of materialism, be it possessions or people, can be strong, yet we must remember that God should always reign supreme in our hearts. He loves us deeply and yearns for our undivided love in return.

PRAYER

Heavenly Father, thank You for waking me up today. There is none other than You. May I always honor You, placing You above all else. **In Jesus' Name, I pray, Amen.**

REFLECTION

As you meditate on today's scripture and lesson, what thoughts or feelings arise? How does this message resonate with your current life circumstances or past experiences? Take a moment to jot down your reflections below.

_____

_____

_____

_____

_____

_____

_____

_____

_____

_____

_____

_____

_____

_____

_____

ACTION

Having reflected on today's message, what tangible steps can you take to apply this lesson in your daily life? Write down one or more actions you intend to take as a response.

DAY 18 - A RELATIONSHIP WITH THE LORD

"Because your love is better than life, my lips will glorify you. I will praise you as long as I live, and in your name, I will lift up my hands."

- Psalms 63:3-4

LIFE LESSON

God is ever-present, always available to hear our prayers and witness our worship. Building a strong relationship with Him isn't just about rituals; it's about frequent conversations, praises, and immersing ourselves in His teachings. A relationship with the Lord provides a foundation that's unshakable, a connection that's eternal.

PRAYER

Heavenly Father, thank You for Your unwavering presence that comforts me. I'm grateful for the bond we share, knowing I can turn to You always. **In Jesus' Name, I pray, Amen.**

REFLECTION

As you meditate on today's scripture and lesson, what thoughts or feelings arise? How does this message resonate with your current life circumstances or past experiences? Take a moment to jot down your reflections below.

_____

_____

_____

_____

_____

_____

_____

_____

_____

_____

_____

_____

_____

_____

_____

_____

_____

_____

ACTION

Having reflected on today's message, what tangible steps can you take to apply this lesson in your daily life? Write down one or more actions you intend to take as a response.

DAY 19 - PRAY

"Pray continually, give thanks in all circumstances; for this is God's will for you in Christ Jesus."

- 1 Thessalonians 5:17-18

LIFE LESSON

In every season of life, during highs and lows, we should never cease to communicate with our Heavenly Father through prayer. Offering gratitude in every circumstance helps us acknowledge His sovereign plan. Remember, prayer doesn't just change circumstances; it transforms hearts.

PRAYER

Heavenly Father, I am grateful for both the blessings and challenges in my journey. They remind me of Your divine purpose and how You form every experience for my growth. **In Jesus' Name, I pray Amen.**

REFLECTION

As you meditate on today's scripture and lesson, what thoughts or feelings arise? How does this message resonate with your current life circumstances or past experiences? Take a moment to jot down your reflections below.

_____

_____

_____

_____

_____

_____

_____

_____

_____

_____

_____

_____

_____

_____

_____

_____

_____

ACTION

Having reflected on today's message, what tangible steps can you take to apply this lesson in your daily life? Write down one or more actions you intend to take as a response.

DAY 20 - SIGNS FROM THE LORD

"Once these signs are fulfilled, do whatever your hand finds for you to do, for God is with you."

- 1 Samuel 10:7

LIFE LESSON

God communicates with us in various ways, often providing signs as guidance or affirmation. These signs may manifest as events, feelings, or even through the words of others. It's essential to remain attentive and discerning to recognize these divine signals and understand His will.

PRAYER

Heavenly Father, grant me the clarity to perceive Your signs and the wisdom to comprehend their meaning. May I always be in tune with Your guidance and move according to Your divine plan. **In Jesus' Name, I pray, Amen.**

REFLECTION

As you meditate on today's scripture and lesson, what thoughts or feelings arise? How does this message resonate with your current life circumstances or past experiences? Take a moment to jot down your reflections below.

_____

_____

_____

_____

_____

_____

_____

_____

_____

_____

_____

_____

_____

_____

_____

_____

_____

ACTION

Having reflected on today's message, what tangible steps can you take to apply this lesson in your daily life? Write down one or more actions you intend to take as a response.

DAY 21 – UNIQUE

"I praise you because I am fearfully and wonderfully made; your works are wonderful; I know that full well."

- Psalms 139:14

LIFE LESSON

Every individual is a masterful creation of God, designed with distinct features, abilities, and a purpose. It's a testament that no two people are the same. Rather than comparing ourselves to others, we should be thankful for the gifts that we are blessed with and embrace the divine purpose for which we were created.

PRAYER

Heavenly Father, I am grateful for the unique way You've created me. May You continue to help me recognize my worth and cherish the qualities You've blessed me with. Guide me to use them for Your glory and honor. **In Jesus' name, I pray, Amen.**

REFLECTION

As you meditate on today's scripture and lesson, what thoughts or feelings arise? How does this message resonate with your current life circumstances or past experiences? Take a moment to jot down your reflections below.

ACTION

Having reflected on today's message, what tangible steps can you take to apply this lesson in your daily life? Write down one or more actions you intend to take as a response.

DAY 22 – PEACE

"I have told you these things so that in me you may have peace. In this world you will have trouble but take heart; I have overcome the world."

- John 16:33

LIFE LESSON

In our journey through life, challenges and difficulties are going to happen. However, in the middle of the storms, Jesus offers a refuge of peace. By grounding ourselves in His teachings and promises, we can navigate through difficulties with grace and tranquility. This peace isn't just the absence of conflict, but the presence of God's assurance and calmness in our hearts.

PRAYER

Heavenly Father, in a world filled with chaos and uncertainties, thank You for being my anchor of peace. Help me to remember that with You by my side, I can face any challenge with a calm heart and confident spirit. **In Jesus' Name, I pray, Amen.**

REFLECTION

As you meditate on today's scripture and lesson, what thoughts or feelings arise? How does this message resonate with your current life circumstances or past experiences? Take a moment to jot down your reflections below.

_____

_____

_____

_____

_____

_____

_____

_____

_____

_____

_____

_____

_____

_____

_____

ACTION

Having reflected on today's message, what tangible steps can you take to apply this lesson in your daily life? Write down one or more actions you intend to take as a response.

DAY 23 – FORGIVENESS

"Bear with each other and forgive one another if any of you has a grievance against someone. Forgive as the Lord forgave you."

- Colossians 3:13

LIFE LESSON

True forgiveness isn't just an action; it's a journey of the heart. We've all been wronged or hurt in some way, and the weight of resentment can become a heavy burden. I recall the pain of betrayal when I was left alone on a day meant for celebration. Yet, in embracing forgiveness, I found a release and a deeper understanding of God's unconditional love for us. When we learn to truly forgive others, the Lord forgives us. Not only do we free ourselves from bitterness, but we also open doors to God's boundless blessings and His infinite mercy.

PRAYER

Heavenly Father, thank You for giving me the strength to forgive even when it felt impossible. Help me to always choose the fruit of the spirit, which is love, joy, peace, forbearance, kindness, goodness, faithfulness, gentleness and self-control. **In Jesus' Name, I pray, Amen.**

REFLECTION

As you meditate on today's scripture and lesson, what thoughts or feelings arise? How does this message resonate with your current life circumstances or past experiences? Take a moment to jot down your reflections below.

_____

_____

_____

_____

_____

_____

_____

_____

_____

_____

_____

_____

_____

_____

_____

_____

_____

_____

ACTION

Having reflected on today's message, what tangible steps can you take to apply this lesson in your daily life? Write down one or more actions you intend to take as a response.

DAY 24 - THE LORD IS EVERYWHERE

"The eyes of the Lord are in every place, beholding the evil and the good."

- Proverbs 15:3

LIFE LESSON

It's a humbling realization that no act, no thought, and no moment is hidden from the sight of the Lord. Often, we find ourselves consumed by the world's perceptions, veiling our actions from the eyes of others, forgetting that God's gaze is omnipresent. The understanding that He witnesses our every act, whether in light or darkness, serves as a reminder to tread the path of righteousness, even when no one's watching.

PRAYER

Heavenly Father, Your ever-watchful eyes remind me to live each day with integrity and truth. Guide me away from temptations and towards a life pleasing in Your sight. **In Jesus' Name, I pray, Amen.**

REFLECTION

As you meditate on today's scripture and lesson, what thoughts or feelings arise? How does this message resonate with your current life circumstances or past experiences? Take a moment to jot down your reflections below.

_____
_____
_____
_____
_____
_____
_____
_____
_____
_____
_____
_____
_____
_____
_____
_____
_____

ACTION

Having reflected on today's message, what tangible steps can you take to apply this lesson in your daily life? Write down one or more actions you intend to take as a response.

DAY 25 - DISTRACTIONS

"Submit yourselves then to God. Resist the devil, and he will flee from you."

- James 4:7

LIFE LESSON

The world is filled with a great number of distractions that can easily lead us astray. The devil is cunning and uses these distractions to lure us away from Jesus' path. It's easy to be tempted, to stray and to forget our divine purpose. But it's crucial to remember that by submitting to the Lord Jesus and steadfastly resisting these temptations, the devil's attempts will be in vain. We hold the power to choose the path of righteousness over fleeting pleasures.

PRAYER

Heavenly Father, thank You for allowing me to resist the lures of the enemy and to remain focused on Your path. Continue to Surround me with physical, emotional and spiritual strength ensuring that I am shielded from all hurt, harm and danger. **In Jesus' Name, I pray, Amen.**

REFLECTION

As you meditate on today's scripture and lesson, what thoughts or feelings arise? How does this message resonate with your current life circumstances or past experiences? Take a moment to jot down your reflections below.

ACTION

Having reflected on today's message, what tangible steps can you take to apply this lesson in your daily life? Write down one or more actions you intend to take as a response.

DAY 26 - HAPPINESS

"For His anger endureth but a moment; in His favour is life. Weeping may endure for a night, but joy cometh in the morning."

- Psalms 30:5

LIFE LESSON

Life has its seasons of sorrow and joy, darkness, and dawn. There will be times when we go through trials and tribulations. However, it's essential to remember that the Lord's grace and favor are enduring, providing a glimmer of hope even in our darkest moments. The tears we shed are often the foundation for the joy that follows. With every challenge faced, we grow stronger in faith, learning to trust Jesus and His greater plan for us.

PRAYER

Heavenly Father, I thank You for Your unfailing love and for bringing me out of situations only You can. Even in my hardest moments, I am comforted by Your promise of a new awakening. I pray that You continue to be that bridge over trouble water. **In Jesus' name, I pray, Amen.**

REFLECTION

As you meditate on today's scripture and lesson, what thoughts or feelings arise? How does this message resonate with your current life circumstances or past experiences? Take a moment to jot down your reflections below.

_____
_____
_____
_____
_____
_____
_____
_____
_____
_____
_____
_____
_____
_____
_____

ACTION

Having reflected on today's message, what tangible steps can you take to apply this lesson in your daily life? Write down one or more actions you intend to take as a response.

DAY 27 - HEAVEN IS REAL

"In my Father's house are many mansions: if it were not so, I would have told you. I go to prepare a place for you. And if I go and prepare a place for you, I will come again and receive you unto myself; that where I am, there ye may be also."

- John 14: 2-3

LIFE LESSON

The promise of Heaven is one of the most comforting truths in the scriptures. It is not just a mythical place, but a promised home for those who walk in faith with the Lord. The love of God extends beyond our earthly existence, offering us eternal life in His presence. Yet, it is important to remember that this promise comes with responsibilities: to accept Jesus Christ, and to live according to God's commandments.

PRAYER

Dear Lord Jesus, continue to keep me on the path of righteousness and guide my heart to always seek You. May my life reflect Your teachings and may I forever remain in Your grace. Help me to be the lady you want to be. **In Jesus' Name, I pray, Amen.**

REFLECTION

As you meditate on today's scripture and lesson, what thoughts or feelings arise? How does this message resonate with your current life circumstances or past experiences? Take a moment to jot down your reflections below.

ACTION

Having reflected on today's message, what tangible steps can you take to apply this lesson in your daily life? Write down one or more actions you intend to take as a response.

DAY 28 - HELL IS REAL

"But the fearful, and unbelieving, and the abominable, and murderers, and whoremongers, and sorcerers, and idolaters, and all liars shall have their part in the lake which burneth with fire and brimstone, which is the second death."

- Revelation 21: 8

LIFE LESSON

The Bible speaks clearly about the consequences of turning away from God's guidance and love. The mention of hell in scriptures serves as a stark reminder of the choices set before us. While God's grace is abundant, He also respects our free will. The flames of hell are not merely symbols, but warnings for us to lead lives aligned with the Lord commandments and to embrace the salvation He offers.

PRAYER

Heavenly Father, every word in Your scriptures is a lesson, a guidance, and a truth. I understand the weight of my choices, and I pray for the strength to always choose the path of righteousness. Protect me from temptation and guide my soul towards eternal life with You. **In Jesus' Name, I pray, Amen.**

REFLECTION

As you meditate on today's scripture and lesson, what thoughts or feelings arise? How does this message resonate with your current life circumstances or past experiences? Take a moment to jot down your reflections below.

ACTION

Having reflected on today's message, what tangible steps can you take to apply this lesson in your daily life? Write down one or more actions you intend to take as a response.

DAY 29 - ENCOURAGEMENT

"May our Lord Jesus Christ himself and God our Father, who loved us and by His grace gave us eternal encouragement and good hope."

- 2 Thessalonians 2:16

LIFE LESSON

We all face moments of doubt and challenge in our lives as we do not live a perfect life such as Jesus. In these moments, let's remember to lift each other up rather than tearing each other down. Encouragement can be a light of hope in someone's storm.

PRAYER

Heavenly Father, teach us to walk by faith and not by sight, resisting all worldly temptations that come to sway us from the path of righteousness. **In Jesus' Name, I pray, Amen.**

REFLECTION

As you meditate on today's scripture and lesson, what thoughts or feelings arise? How does this message resonate with your current life circumstances or past experiences? Take a moment to jot down your reflections below.

_____
_____
_____
_____
_____
_____
_____
_____
_____
_____
_____
_____
_____
_____
_____
_____
_____

ACTION

Having reflected on today's message, what tangible steps can you take to apply this lesson in your daily life? Write down one or more actions you intend to take as a response.

_____

_____

_____

_____

_____

_____

_____

_____

_____

_____

_____

_____

_____

_____

_____

DAY 30 - SALVATION

"If you declare with your mouth 'Jesus is Lord,' and believe in your heart that God raised Him from the dead, you will be saved."

- Romans 10:9

LIFE LESSON

Since embracing salvation, I've experienced a renewed sense of purpose and joy. This doesn't mean life is free from challenges; it simply means that I have chosen to walk with Jesus through them rather than without Him. My commitment to Christ is the anchor amidst life's storms.

PRAYER

Heavenly Father, I'm deeply grateful for the gift of salvation. Continue to lead and guide me, ensuring my path aligns with Your will. **In Jesus' Name, I pray, Amen.**

REFLECTION

As you meditate on today's scripture and lesson, what thoughts or feelings arise? How does this message resonate with your current life circumstances or past experiences? Take a moment to jot down your reflections below.

_____

_____

_____

_____

_____

_____

_____

_____

_____

_____

_____

_____

_____

_____

_____

_____

_____

ACTION

Having reflected on today's message, what tangible steps can you take to apply this lesson in your daily life? Write down one or more actions you intend to take as a response.

COMMITMENT AND RECOMMITMENT

As you take hold of new life in Jesus Christ, reflect on the insights, growth, and transformations you've experienced on this 30-day journey. While this book may conclude, your spiritual journey should not. Continue to strive for a closer walk and a deeper understanding in the faith. Revisit these teachings daily and even monthly, as these lessons may help with reference points for scripture interpretation. Trust and believe His word!

"So shall my word that goeth forth out of my mouth: it shall not return unto me void, but it shall accomplish that which I please, and it shall prosper in the thing whereto I sent it."

- Isaiah 55:11

ACKNOWLEDGMENTS

First giving honor to God Almighty, whose wisdom, guidance, and love have been my constant beacon of light during the journey of penning this book. To my family, for their unwavering support and love, always encouraging me to pursue my dreams and never stop believing. Their faith in my mission has often been the fuel to keep me moving forward.

To my friends, who listened to my ideas, provided feedback, and acted as my sounding board, offering both praise and constructive criticism. I cherish our moments of deep reflection and hearty laughter.

Special thanks to GeeMorgan Publishing, for their meticulous editing, patience, and dedication to ensuring this book was presented in its best form.

To the countless authors and spiritual leaders who came before me, whose teachings and writings have paved the way for my own journey and understanding.

Lastly, to YOU, the reader. Without you, these words would remain silent on pages. I hope that in reading this, you find the inspiration, strength, and the guidance you seek.

In gratitude and love,

Erica Moss

Made in the USA
Middletown, DE
11 December 2023